Dear Parent:

Congratulations! Your child is taking the first steps on an exciting journey. The destination? Independent reading!

STEP INTO READING® will help your child get there. The program offers five steps to reading success. Each step includes fun stories and colorful art. There are also Step into Reading Sticker Books, Step into Reading Math Readers, Step into Reading Phonics Readers, Step into Reading Write-In Readers, and Step into Reading Phonics Boxed Sets—a complete literacy program with something to interest every child.

Learning to Read, Step by Step!

Ready to Read   Preschool–Kindergarten
• big type and easy words • rhyme and rhythm • picture clues
For children who know the alphabet and are eager to begin reading.

Reading with Help   Preschool–Grade 1
• basic vocabulary • short sentences • simple stories
For children who recognize familiar words and sound out new words with help.

Reading on Your Own   Grades 1–3
• engaging characters • easy-to-follow plots • popular topics
For children who are ready to read on their own.

Reading Paragraphs   Grades 2–3
• challenging vocabulary • short paragraphs • exciting stories
For newly independent readers who read simple sentences with confidence.

Ready for Chapters   Grades 2–4
• chapters • longer paragraphs • full-color art
For children who want to take the plunge into chapter books but still like colorful pictures.

STEP INTO READING® is designed to give every child a successful reading experience. The grade levels are only guides. Children can progress through the steps at their own speed, developing confidence in their reading, no matter what their grade.

Remember, a lifetime love of reading starts with a single step!

STEP INTO READING®

Featuring characters from your favorite **Disney** and **Disney·PIXAR** movies!

Tales of Fun & Friendship

Step 1 and Step 2 Books
A Collection of Six Early Readers

Random House 🏠 New York

Contents

STEP INTO READING®

STEP 1

Disney · PIXAR

TOY STORY 2

Me Too, Woody!

By Heidi Kilgras

Illustrated by Atelier Philippe Harchy

Random House 🏠 New York

Buzz and Woody.

Good buddies!

Game time.

Checkers!

"Me too, Woody!"

"No, only two."

Buzz and Woody.

Good buddies!

Playtime.

Seesaw!

"Me too, Woody!"

"No, only two."

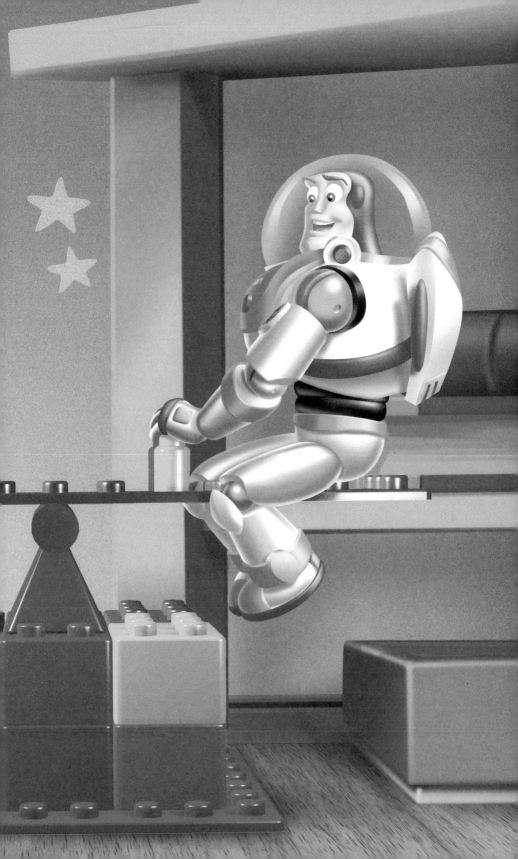

Poor Jessie!

"Hey, Jessie."

"Want to play?"

"Yay!"

Play ball!

Big swing.

Big hit!

"Run, Buzz!"

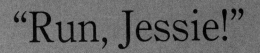

"Run, Jessie!"

Going.
Going.

Got it!

Good play!
Good buddies!

DISNEY · PIXAR

FINDING NEMO

Just Keep Swimming

By Melissa Lagonegro

Illustrated by Atelier Philippe Harchy

Random House 🏠 New York

Nemo has a dream.
He wants to join
the school swim team.

But Nemo has
a little fin.

He thinks that
he will never win.

Dory helps Nemo.

She teaches him
to go, go, go!

Nemo races and races.

Nemo chases and chases.

"Just keep swimming,"
Dory sings.

But Nemo thinks
of other things.

"I will never win.

I have a bad fin."

"Just keep swimming!"
Dory cries.

So Nemo tries . . .

and tries . . .

. . . and tries.

Nemo races and races.

Nemo chases and chases.

Yippee! Yahoo!

His dream comes true.

Nemo makes the team.

Can Nemo win the
first-place prize?

"Just keep swimming!"
Dory cries.

Watch him race.

Watch him chase.

Watch as Nemo wins
first place!

STEP INTO READING®

By Monica Kulling

Illustrated by Denise Shimabukuro and
the Disney Storybook Artists

Designed by Disney's Global Design Group

Random House 🏠 New York

Lilo waved to Myrtle.

She wanted to be

Myrtle's friend.

"I got a new dog!"

Lilo yelled.

"His name is Stitch."

Myrtle rode up
on her new trike.
"Wow!" said Myrtle.
"That dog is ugly."
Stitch made a face.

Stitch was <u>not</u> a dog.

He was blue and furry.

He had big ears.

And he had sharp teeth.

Stitch was really

an alien!

Pleakley and Jumba
were aliens, too.

They had come to Earth
to catch Stitch.
Pleakley tripped over
Jumba's foot.
"Whoa!" said Pleakley.

Stitch saw Pleakley.

Then he saw Jumba.

He had to get away!

Stitch had an idea.

He grabbed
Myrtle's trike.

He grabbed Lilo's hand.

They took off!

Stitch rode fast!

"Hey!" yelled Myrtle.

"Oh, no!" said Pleakley.
"Stitch is getting away!"

"Grab that scooter!"
said Jumba.
"We will catch him!"

Lilo and Stitch rode
under a waterfall.
Splash!

They got all wet.

But Lilo did not care.

"Cool!" she cried.

Jumba and Pleakley
rode under
the waterfall.
They got soaked.

They did not like it
one bit!

Stitch came to a cliff.
There was nowhere to go.
Just lots and lots
of water.

Stitch turned right.

Lilo hung on tight.

Jumba and Pleakley
zoomed right into
the water!
Lucky for them,
someone was surfing!

Lilo and Stitch
zoomed right
through a market!
"Yum!" said Lilo.

"Ooof!" said Pleakley.
Jumba drove into
a bunch of bananas!

Stitch rode past
a volcano.

It began to rumble.

Smoke and

lava came out.

"Uh-oh!" said Lilo.

"Go, Stitch, go!"

Stitch rode faster.

"We have him now,"
said Jumba.
The aliens
were getting closer.

But so was
the lava!

Jumba and Pleakley
jumped off the scooter.
They climbed a tree.

And Lilo and Stitch
got away!

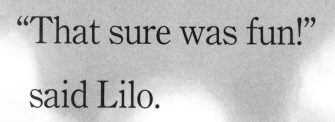

"That sure was fun!"

said Lilo.

"Let's do it again!"

STEP INTO READING®

THE KOALA KING

By Apple Jordan

Illustrated by the Disney Storybook Artists

Random House 🏠 New York

Nigel is a koala.

He lives in the zoo.

Toy koalas are cuddly.

But Nigel is not a toy.

He does not like

being cuddly.

He wants to be

big and strong.

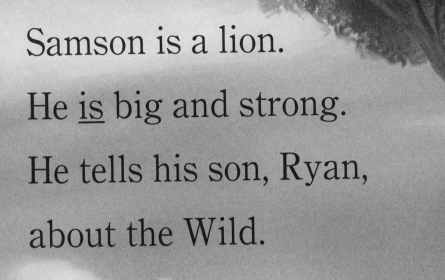

Samson is a lion.

He <u>is</u> big and strong.

He tells his son, Ryan,

about the Wild.

One day,
Ryan was taken
to the Wild.

Samson had to get
Ryan back.

Nigel and his friends
wanted to go, too.
Samson told them
it would not be safe.
But they had to help.

The gang set sail
for the Wild.
They had to find Ryan.

The trip was
long and hard.
Nigel was hot.
Nigel was hungry.

Nigel was fed up.

He jumped

off the boat.

Nigel hit land.
They reached
the Wild at last!

The gang went
in search of Ryan.
But Nigel fell behind.
He was on his own.

Nigel met a pack
of beasts
in the Wild.

They bowed
down to him.
They were happy
to see him.

Long ago
a toy koala
had fallen
from the sky.

The toy saved the beasts
from hungry lions.
It was a sign
that one day
the beasts would rule.

Now a real koala
had come to the beasts.
The beasts thought
Nigel would help
them rule the Wild.

They made him
their king.
Nigel liked being king.

The beasts found some
of Nigel's friends.
They even found Ryan!

But the beasts wanted
to cook his friends.
Nigel had to think fast.

Samson showed up
just in time!
Nigel needed help.
They made a plan
to save the gang.

Nigel tricked
the beasts.
He faked a fight
with Samson.

It worked!

The gang got away.

They even made

some new friends.

Nigel saved the day!

The friends headed
home at last.

Nigel threw
the cuddly toy away
once and for all.
He proved that he was
one big strong koala.

Disney's **chicken little**

The Sky Is Falling!

By Apple Jordan

Illustrated by the Disney Storybook Artists

Designed by Disney Publishing's Global Design Group

Random House 🏠 New York

Chicken Little
made a big mistake.
He rang the town bell
to warn everyone
that the sky
was falling.

But the sky never fell.
His dad, Buck, said
it was only an acorn.

Everyone teased
Chicken Little.
No one would let him
forget his mistake.

Chicken Little was tired
of being teased.
He wanted
things to change.
"Today is a new day,"
he said.

Chicken Little joined
the baseball team.
"Maybe my luck
will change,"
he thought.

His luck did change!

He hit a home run.

He won the big game!

Chicken Little
was happy.
His dad was proud.
Things were better.

But then
there was trouble.
The sky really did fall
on Chicken Little!
A piece landed
right in his bedroom.

Fish, Abby, and Runt
came to help him.
Fish picked up
the piece of sky.
It floated in the air.
It flew out the window.
Fish flew out with it!

The friends raced
to help Fish.
They saw a spaceship
in the sky.

The friends snuck
onto the spaceship.
Fish was there!
And they learned that
Earth was in danger.
They had to tell
someone!

Chicken Little ran
to the school.
He rang the bell.
<u>Ding!</u> <u>Dong!</u>
"Aliens!" he cried.
"Aliens are here!"

Everyone thought
Chicken Little
was crazy.
Even his dad.

But soon Buck

saw it for himself.

The sky was

falling apart!

Chicken Little saw
an alien kid running.
He knew he was lost.

He had to return
the alien kid
to his parents.

Buck and Chicken Little
faced the aliens.

The Earth was not
in danger after all.
The aliens were only
looking for their child.

Chicken Little
gave the alien kid
back to his family.

Now the aliens
could go home.
Chicken Little
was a hero!

157

Things had changed after all!

The Great Toy Escape

By Kitty Richards

Illustrated by Caroline Egan, Adrienne Brown,
Scott Tilley, and Studio IBOIX

Random House 🏠 New York

Andy's toys love
to play.
But Andy is grown up.
He does not play
with his toys
anymore.

The toys must find
a new home.
They climb
into a car.

The car goes
to Sunnyside Daycare.

Sunnyside is full
of toys!

A bear named Lotso is
in charge.

There are kids
at Sunnyside every day.
Andy's toys are happy.
The kids will play
with them!

But Woody is not happy.

He misses Andy.

He leaves.

It is time to play!

The little kids pull.

They throw.

They yell.

The toys do not like it.

The toys want
to go home.
But the door is locked!

Lotso is mean.

He will not let

Andy's toys leave.

Lotso and his gang lock
up Andy's toys!

Then Woody comes back.

He has a plan.

They will escape!

That night,
Woody and Slinky
steal the key!

The toys sneak outside.
They do not
make a sound.

The toys try to escape.

Oh, no!

They fall

into a garbage truck.

The truck goes
to the dump.
The toys are
in danger!
They must escape.

They run!
Woody tells them
to hurry.
They look
for a way out.

They slide!
The toys hold hands
to stay together.

184

At last,

they escape!

The toys hide
in the garbage.
They go back
to Andy's house.

The toys are safe.

They are happy

to be home.

Andy finds his toys
a new owner.
She loves to play!
And the toys love
their new home.